This

Book

belongs to

"It has been my pleasure and delight to review Patsy Henry's new book, *My Hare Line Meets the Brown Rabbit*. I found the book to be well-written, and it gives an insight that certain places and people can be much better and safer than first perceived."

-Saralyn D. Swicord
Retired Magistrate, Bainbridge, GA

Published by Tate Publishing & Enterprises, LLC
127 E. Trade Center Terrace | Mustang, Oklahoma 73064 USA
1.888.361.9473 | www.tatepublishing.com

Tate Publishing is committed to excellence in the publishing industry. The company reflects
the philosophy established by the founders, based on Psalm 68:11,
"The Lord gave the word and great was the company of those who published it."

Book design copyright © 2009 by Tate Publishing, LLC. All rights reserved.
Cover and Interior design by Elizabeth A. Mason
Illustrations by Katie Brooks
Photographs by Jerry T. Henry

Published in the United States of America

ISBN: 978-1-60799-357-5
1. Juvenile Fiction: Animals: Rabbits
2. Juvenile Fiction: Nature & the Natural World: Environment
09.03.19

My HARE Line meets the Brown Rabbit

book 2 of the series by Patsy M. Henry

TATE PUBLISHING & Enterprises

My Hare Line Meets the Brown Rabbit was written in memory of Melissa Weaver Donley, who passed away May 13, 2008, at the age of thirty-eight from metastatic squamous cell carcinoma. This photo was taken on April 15, 2006. Starting from the right is Greg, Melissa, Coy, and Hilary.

Acknowledgments

I want to express my sincere appreciation to my husband and best friend, Jerry, for reading my manuscripts over and over again. He offered suggestions that have been helpful, and he has been my biggest critic. I could not have done this without him.

Also, special thanks to my sisters, Betty Thrift, Anita Kendrick, Bobbie Kearns, Wanda Price, and Audrey Streat for all of their encouragement.

Last, but not least, I want to thank my son, Greg Donley, for having faith in me and encouraging me to follow my dream and write my story.

fOREWORd

Humans seldom think about how our desires to sustain the twenty-first-century lifestyle affect the natural environment. Every now and then, a person comes along who helps us to see our passions in a different light.

I am convinced God gives insight to a special few, like Patsy Henry, who send us gentle reminders of how our swift actions to create bigger and better reap havoc on native habitats. The building of new subdivisions, shopping malls, and roadways leaves more than a few animals homeless.

As an animal lover, Patsy's story gives us a very real insight into the loss of wildlife habitat. Wildlife creatures become homeless not only from cutting forests, but also from the clearing of brush, shrubs, and trees in backyards, the birthplaces and homes of generations of wildlife. In *My Hare Line Meets the Brown Rabbit,* the natural fear animals have of humans is so skillfully expressed.

More than ever, wildlife must adapt in an environment where pets and human encroachment injure or orphan young wildlife as this story so aptly reveals. Unlike the author, too many of us lack the insight and compassion for the beloved creatures that live in our neighborhoods! After all, this world is home to them too.

Psalm 50:10 reads, "For every beast of the forest is mine, and the cattle on a thousand hills." When God gave us dominion over the animals, he expected us to handle this responsibility well and give all of his creation the opportunity to thrive. In Matthew 10: 29, Jesus tells us that God knows even when a sparrow drops to the ground.

Children will love this story. Through reading or hearing it, perhaps the next generation will make wiser choices than previous ones. The narrative fosters repeated reading because it touches the heart.

The framework of the story was born out of the author's real-life experiences with her own beloved rabbits and a daughter-in-law who fought cancer valiantly up to the very end of her short life. Mother Theresa once expressed that the love in us must be willing to give until it hurts so that we can bring justice and peace to those around us. The content portrays so well how the future of wildlife lies in our hands.

Because of the storyline, just maybe, the next generation will work harder to protect wildlife and not compromise the least of these.

Marjean Boyd
Retired Educator, Bainbridge, GA

Brownie and Granddad lived just outside a small South Georgia town. During recent months, a large shopping mall had been built right down the road from the forest they called their home. Now, much to their sorrow, the giant orange machines that pushed the trees up were parked just at the edge of the woods. Soon they would be forced to find another home. Granddad sent word for Jay to come at once. Jay was his best friend, and Granddad knew he could handle his request.

"What we feared most is about to happen!" Granddad said to Jay when he came. "You must take Brownie to safety at once. Use the evacuation route we mapped out together."

"I'm on it!" exclaimed Jay. "We'll leave right away."

Brownie hugged Granddad and told him she would miss him. She asked him to say goodbye to her best friend, Phil Mouse, for her. Granddad stayed behind so he could help all their friends find safe places to live. Brownie and Jay departed just after the orange ball disappeared behind the trees. They headed straight across the hard path the humans raced down all day long in their cars.

EVACUATION
THIS WAY

Brownie was sad that she had to leave and find a new home, but she knew she just had to be brave! They passed by several houses the humans lived in. Jay asked Brownie to go through a huge tunnel next to one of the houses. He flew above the tunnel and met her at the end. It was pretty dark in there. On the other side, there were more houses.

"How much farther?" Brownie asked.

"Be patient, Brownie, we'll be there soon," replied Jay.

Brownie hopped and Jay flew ahead of her to make sure there were no dogs or humans around. He had to take good care of Brownie. His best friend was counting on him. They approached a hill and Jay said, "Brownie, be careful going up this hill. We're almost there now."

Brownie looked down after reaching the top of the hill, but she could not see her old home. She turned to follow Jay and was shocked to see a big house.

"That's not your home," Jay said. "You'll be living near the house under the holly bushes. My friend, Mary Wren, has a nest nearby, and she will keep you safe."

"This looks like a great place to live," said Brownie. "Thank you for taking such good care of me."

"You're welcome. You get settled in, and tomorrow I will show you where I live," said Jay.

It was strange for Brownie to go to sleep without Granddad there to say goodnight.

The next morning Brownie heard the birds singing. Mary Wren alerted Jay to let him know Brownie was awake. Jay invited Brownie to come into the backyard. He said, "Mr. and Mrs. Warden live in the big house. Mrs. Warden keeps sunflower seeds in this feeder and water in the birdbath. I live in this azalea bush nearby. You'll like the Wardens. They are our friends."

Then Brownie spotted it. It was huge! She had heard about prison camps from Granddad. It had a tall fence and inside there were cages. All of a sudden, Mr. Warden came out of the big house.

Jay said, "Just sit still. He won't see you because you will blend in with the pine straw."

Mr. Warden entered the prison camp and opened the cages. The rabbits jumped out of the cages one by one. That was strange! They didn't act like they were scared of him. Brownie had been taught by Granddad to hide when humans were around. She decided to keep a close eye on them.

Jay told her, "The rabbits let the Wardens pet them. Why, my dad told me that Mrs. Warden used to take Paula Rabbit into the big house to play when her grandchildren, Hilary and Coy, came for a visit."

Brownie asked, "Do Hilary and Coy come to visit often?"

"No, not as much. Their mother, Melissa, got really sick. I heard Mrs. Warden talking about it to Mr. Warden. She used to go take care of Hilary and Coy when their dad took their mom to the doctor," Jay explained.

Brownie said, "I hope they can help Melissa get well."

Jay said, "It's so sad. They didn't find out how to make her better, and she died not long ago. Mrs. Warden cried. Now Mrs. Warden visits Hilary and Coy to help out with things at their home."

It was around four p.m., and Mrs. Warden headed for the rabbit pen with apples, carrots, and grapes. She didn't have to tell the rabbits it was snack time. The minute they heard the rustling sound from the plastic grocery bag, they headed inside to get their treats.

All of a sudden, Mrs. Warden had a feeling she was being watched. She turned around slowly and looked to the left. There was no one there. She turned to the right and did not see anyone at first. After a moment, she spotted a little brown rabbit near the birdbath. The rabbit didn't move. It appeared to be watching her.

"Jay, I thought you said she couldn't see me," said Brownie. "She's looking straight at me."

"You're wrong. Just sit still. She's looking at the roses," answered Jay.

Mrs. Warden continued to give the rabbits their treats. She talked to them and called them by name. She said, "Hey, Paula Rabbit, how's my big girl today? I brought green grapes this time. I hope they are as good as they look. Snowball, come get some of the grapes before they are all gone."

Mrs. Warden left the rabbit pen and was surprised to see that the little brown rabbit was still sitting near the birdbath. She decided to give her a treat also. She went inside the house and brought out a plastic container. When she came back outside, the rabbit was not there. Mrs. Warden decided to go ahead and put a couple of grapes in the container, and she placed it under an azalea bush near the birdbath.

The next day, Mrs. Warden checked, and the grapes were not in the plastic container. She put a couple of grapes there again. Later, Mrs. Warden told Mr. Warden about leaving grapes for the little brown rabbit.

A couple of days later Mrs. Warden was sitting on the back porch watching the rabbits play. Much to her surprise, she saw the brown rabbit eating the grapes out of the container. She could hardly believe her eyes. That very afternoon Mrs. Warden put rabbit pellets in a container right outside the pen just to see what would happen. The next day some of the rabbit pellets were gone. Several days later, Mrs. Warden saw the little brown rabbit eating the rabbit pellets. "This is unbelievable!" Mrs. Warden said.

Brownie was enjoying the grapes and the rabbit pellets, but she was still going to keep a close eye out. She remembered Granddad had taught her to hide when humans were around.

Days passed and Brownie came and went all around the neighborhood. She always returned to the Wardens' yard. She had started to count on having rabbit pellets and grapes.

One day, Brownie suddenly heard a loud noise. It sounded like it was coming from above in the next pen. Brownie had figured out that she could easily hop in and out of the rabbit pens without the Wardens' help. After a moment, she realized the bunny Mrs. Warden called Paula Rabbit was stamping her foot. That's when she saw them. "These must be the monster dogs Jay told me about," said Brownie. They were trying to dig under the fence. The rabbits ran down into a hole in the ground in their pen. Brownie had not noticed the hole before now. About that time, Mr. and Mrs. Warden came out and chased the dogs away. "Boy, was that a close call!" exclaimed Brownie.

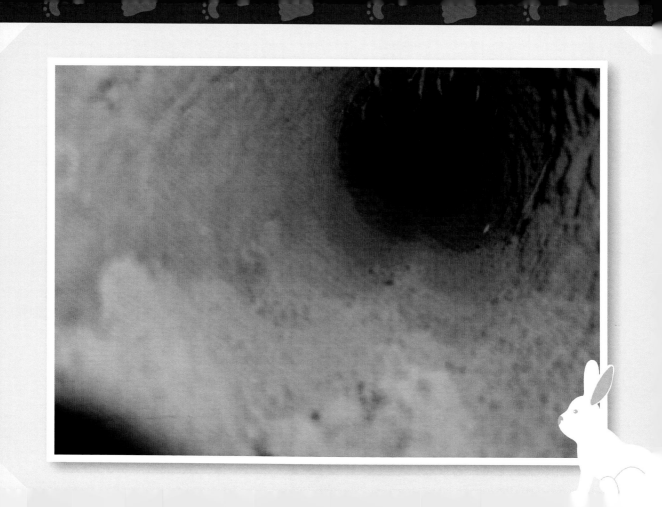

After the dogs left, the rabbits came back out of the hole. Brownie decided to get a closer look at the big hole. "Wow," she said to the rest of the rabbits. "I bet it took a long time to dig this hole. Thank goodness Paula Rabbit gave the warning signal. That gave you time to run down into the hole for safety. I'm glad Mr. and Mrs. Warden chased the dogs away. You are lucky that they take such good care of you. "

Paula Rabbit and the others stared straight ahead in the direction the dogs had run. They did not answer Brownie. She decided they must not be able to hear her or see her. Brownie said, "I guess my brown fur blends in with the ground and they can't see me, just like the Wardens!"

EPILOGUE

I walked around our neighborhood recently and during that walk I saw two brown rabbits in a yard. Truly, wildlife has relocated because of the construction at a major highway near our home. As a result, Brownie made her move to our yard. She has added joy to our lives, and that is what *My Hare Line Meets the Brown Rabbit* is all about. It has been funny to me that the pet rabbits never acknowledge the presence of Brownie. She appears to be invisible to them. I have found that talking to the rabbits seems to make them relax, and they don't appear to feel threatened. Thus, I have talked to Brownie as well. As she spends more time in our yard, she has learned to trust us at a distance.

Follow along as Brownie makes herself at home. Watch for more *My Hare Line* books to keep up with these curious, lovable pets.

listen|imagine|view|experience

AUDIO BOOK DOWNLOAD INCLUDED WITH THIS BOOK!

In your hands you hold a complete digital entertainment package. Besides purchasing the paper version of this book, this book includes a free download of the audio version of this book. Simply use the code listed below when visiting our website. Once downloaded to your computer, you can listen to the book through your computer's speakers, burn it to an audio CD or save the file to your portable music device (such as Apple's popular iPod) and listen on the go!

How to get your free audio book digital download:

1. Visit www.tatepublishing.com and click on the e|LIVE logo on the home page.
2. Enter the following coupon code:
    cdae-9a08-b1a2-4442-402e-7006-f623-8339
3. Download the audio book from your e|LIVE digital locker and begin enjoying your new digital entertainment package today!